CHAPTERS

D0179746

CHAPTER ONE
FUN . . . AND NOT FUN

One sunny morning, a little mouse named Ricky Ricotta went out to play with his giant Mighty Robot.

First, they came to the playground.

The Mighty Robot pushed Ricky
on the swing set.
"This is fun," said Ricky.

Then Ricky tried to push his Robot
on the swing set.

"This is not fun," said Ricky.

Next, Ricky and his Robot flew
to the amusement park.
Ricky got on the Ferris wheel.
"This is fun!" said Ricky.

Then Ricky's Mighty Robot got on
the Ferris wheel.
"This is not fun," said Ricky.

Finally, Ricky and his Mighty
Robot went to the swimming pool.
Ricky did a perfect swan dive.
"That was fun!" said Ricky.

Then Ricky's Robot jumped in, too.

All of the water splashed out of the pool.

"That was *NOT FUN*," said Ricky.

CHAPTER TWO
THE WISH

Ricky and his Mighty Robot walked
home. Ricky was not happy.

That night after supper, Ricky's
Mighty Robot helped Ricky get
ready for bed.

Usually Ricky enjoyed brushing
his teeth with the Turbo-Toothbrush
built into his Robot's index finger . . .

. . . but not tonight.

Usually Ricky laughed when his Robot
helped him put on his pajamas . . .

. . . but not tonight.

And usually Ricky had fun when
his Robot tucked him into bed . . .

. . . but not tonight.

Ricky loved his Mighty Robot, but sometimes it was hard having a best friend who was so *BIG*.

"I wish my Mighty Robot had somebody his own size to play with," Ricky whispered. "Then maybe I could have fun by myself."

As Ricky went to sleep that evening, he did not suspect that his wish was about to come true.

CHAPTER THREE
UNCLE UNICORN

At that very moment, about 1,650 million miles away on a planet called Uranus, a nasty creature named Uncle Unicorn was hatching a hideous plan.

Uncle Unicorn was the president
of Unicorp Inc. He had made a lot
of money by turning his planet into
a nuclear dumping ground.

All over the galaxy, creatures
came to unload their toxic waste
onto Uranus.

Most of the Unicorns who lived on Uranus had moved away a long time ago. But the three who remained had mutated into gigantic Uranium Unicorns, and they served their evil boss with glee.

That night, Uncle Unicorn looked
out at his planet through the window
of his tall office building. "I've
destroyed my entire planet," he laughed.
"Now I shall take over the Earth."

Uncle Unicorn knew about Ricky's Mighty Robot. He knew that the evilest minds in the galaxy had tried to fight Ricky's Robot and failed.

"But I've got a trick that's SURE to stop Ricky Ricotta's Mighty Robot once and for all!" snarled Uncle Unicorn.

Uncle Unicorn took his three
Uranium Unicorns into his rocket
ship and blasted off toward Earth.

CHAPTER FOUR
THE LADYBOT

The next day, Ricky ran outside to wake up his Mighty Robot.

"Mighty Robot!" cried Ricky. "You got a present! You got a present!"

Ricky's Robot threw off his
pajamas and ran to see the giant
present.

"I wonder who it is from,"
said Ricky.

Ricky's Mighty Robot opened
up the present.
Inside was a giant Ladybot.
She was big and pink, and she
had a giant heart on her chest.

Suddenly, the heart began to glow
and a laser beam shot out. It zapped
Ricky's Robot right in his eyes.

"Hey!" shouted Ricky. "What's the
big idea?"

The giant heart stopped glowing,
and the Ladybot returned to normal.
But Ricky's Mighty Robot was not
normal anymore. He had changed.
He had a funny look in his eyes.
He was *in LOVE*!

The Ladybot held out her hand,
and Ricky's Mighty Robot took it.
Then, together, the two Robots turned
and skipped away down the street.
BOOM! BOOM! BOOM!
"Mighty Robot!" called Ricky.
"Come back here!"
But Ricky's Mighty Robot was gone.

CHAPTER FIVE
ALONE

Ricky tried to follow his Mighty
Robot, but he could not keep up.

"Hey, wait for me!" Ricky called.

But the two Robots did not wait.

Ricky was all alone.

That night, Ricky's Mighty Robot
did not come home for supper.

He was not there to help Ricky
brush his teeth . . .

. . . or put on his pajamas . . .

. . . or tuck him into bed.

"Would you like us to tuck you in tonight?" asked Ricky's parents.

"No, thank you," said Ricky. And he went to sleep with a sad heart.

CHAPTER SIX
THE NEXT DAY

The next day, Ricky went looking for
his Mighty Robot. He searched all
over town, but he could not find his
Robot anywhere.

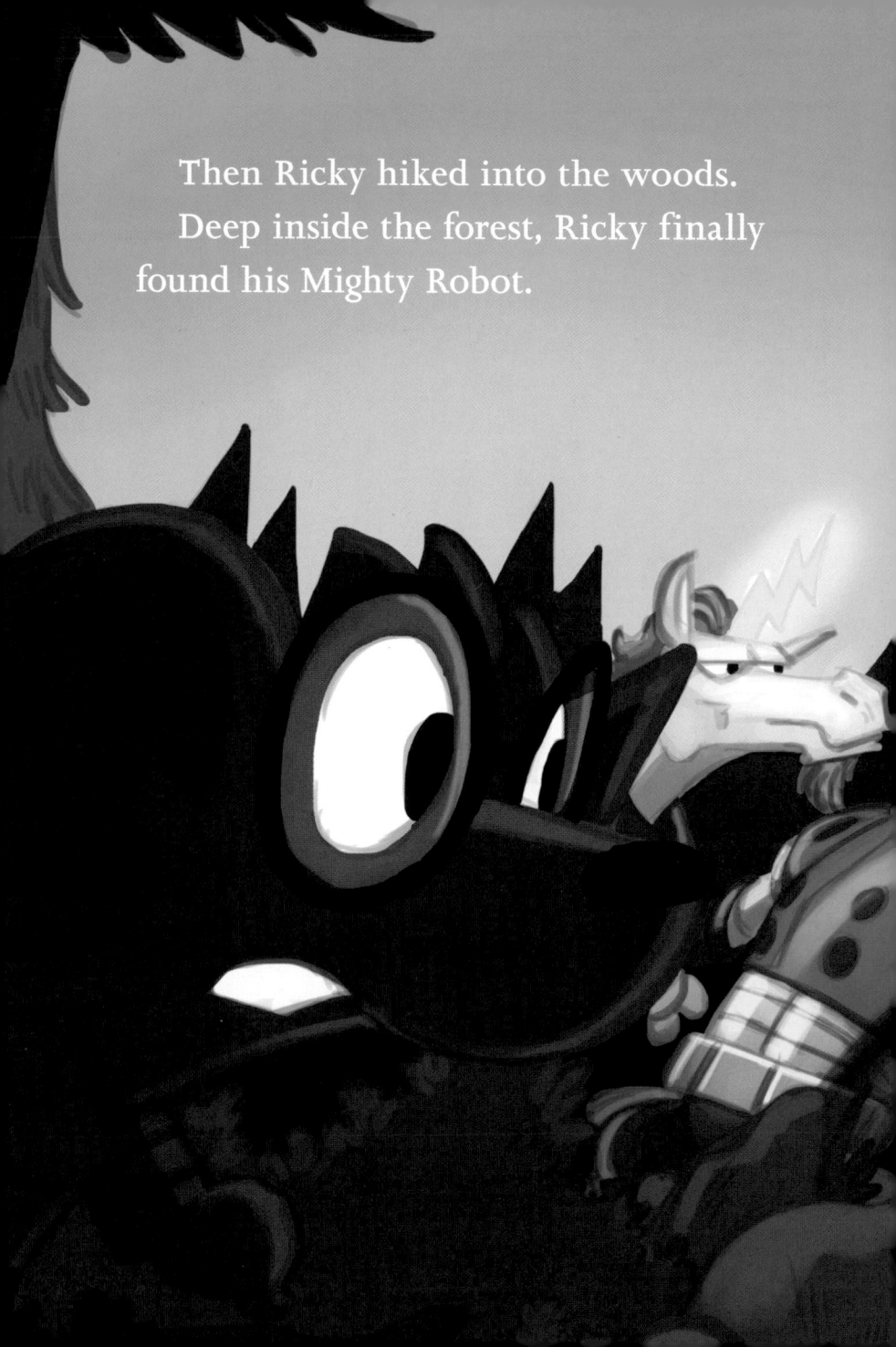

Then Ricky hiked into the woods. Deep inside the forest, Ricky finally found his Mighty Robot.

But as he got closer, Ricky discovered something horrible. His Mighty Robot had been captured.

"A-*HA!*" said Ricky. "I *KNEW* that Ladybot was up to no good!" Suddenly, the Ladybot's giant heart opened up, and Uncle Unicorn peeked out.

Now that we've got that Mighty Robot under the spell of our evil Hypno-Ray," said Uncle Unicorn, "he won't be able to stop our terrible plans! But just to be on the safe side, I want you Uranium Unicorns to DESTROY him!"

"OH, NO!" gasped Ricky. "I've got to save my Mighty Robot!"

CHAPTER SEVEN
HELP IS ON THE WAY

Ricky ran back through the woods and all the way to the other side of town. Finally, he reached his cousin Lucy's house.

Lucy was in the backyard playing with her pet Jurassic Jackrabbits, Fudgie, Cupcake, and Waffles.

"Hi, Ricky," said Lucy. "Do you want to play *princess?*"

"*NO!*" cried Ricky, panting hard and out of breath. "I . . . NEED . . . TO . . . BORROW . . . WAFFLES!"

"Come on, Waffles," said Lucy.
"This looks like an emergency!"
Lucy and Ricky climbed onto
Waffles's back and prepared
for takeoff.

Fudgie and Cupcake wanted
to help, too, but Lucy told them
to stay home.

AW, YOU GUYS FEEL LEFT OUT, DON'TCHA?

HMMM...

I'VE GOT IT!

YOU TWO HAVE A VERY IMPORTANT JOB TODAY!

I NEED YOU TO STAY HERE AND GUARD THESE COOKIES!

CHAPTER EIGHT
INSIDE THE LADYBOT

Soon, Ricky, Lucy, and Waffles reached the woods. There they saw Ricky's Mighty Robot being held by the Uranium Unicorns.

"My Mighty Robot has been hypnotized," said Ricky. "And those evil Unicorn guys are going to destroy him!"

"But what can we do?" asked Lucy.

"We've got to stop that giant Ladybot now!" said Ricky. "She's controlling my Robot with a Hypno-Ray!"

Waffles landed carefully on the Ladybot's shoulder.

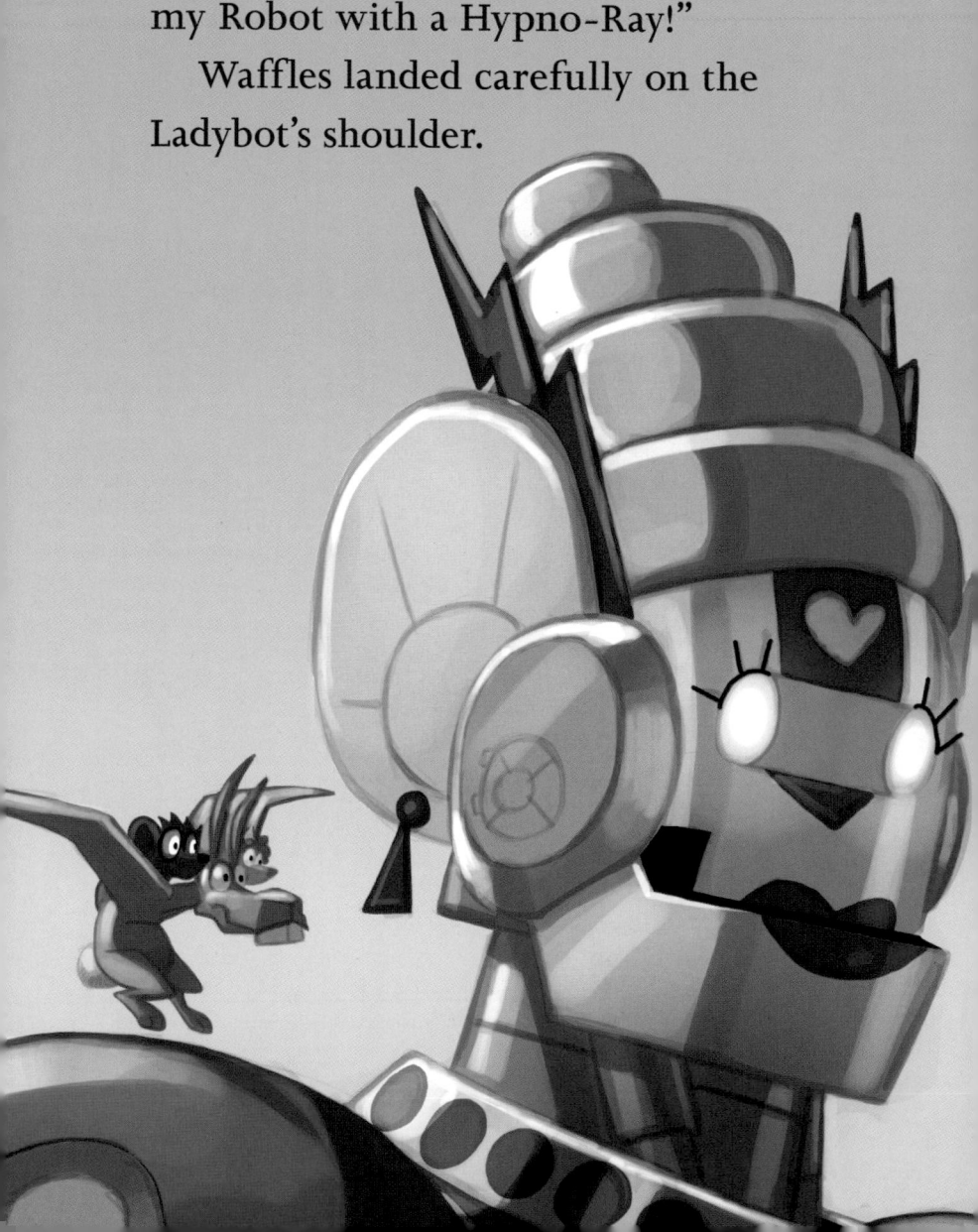

Ricky and Lucy climbed into
the Ladybot's cheek and looked
around for a way
to turn off the
Hypno-Ray.

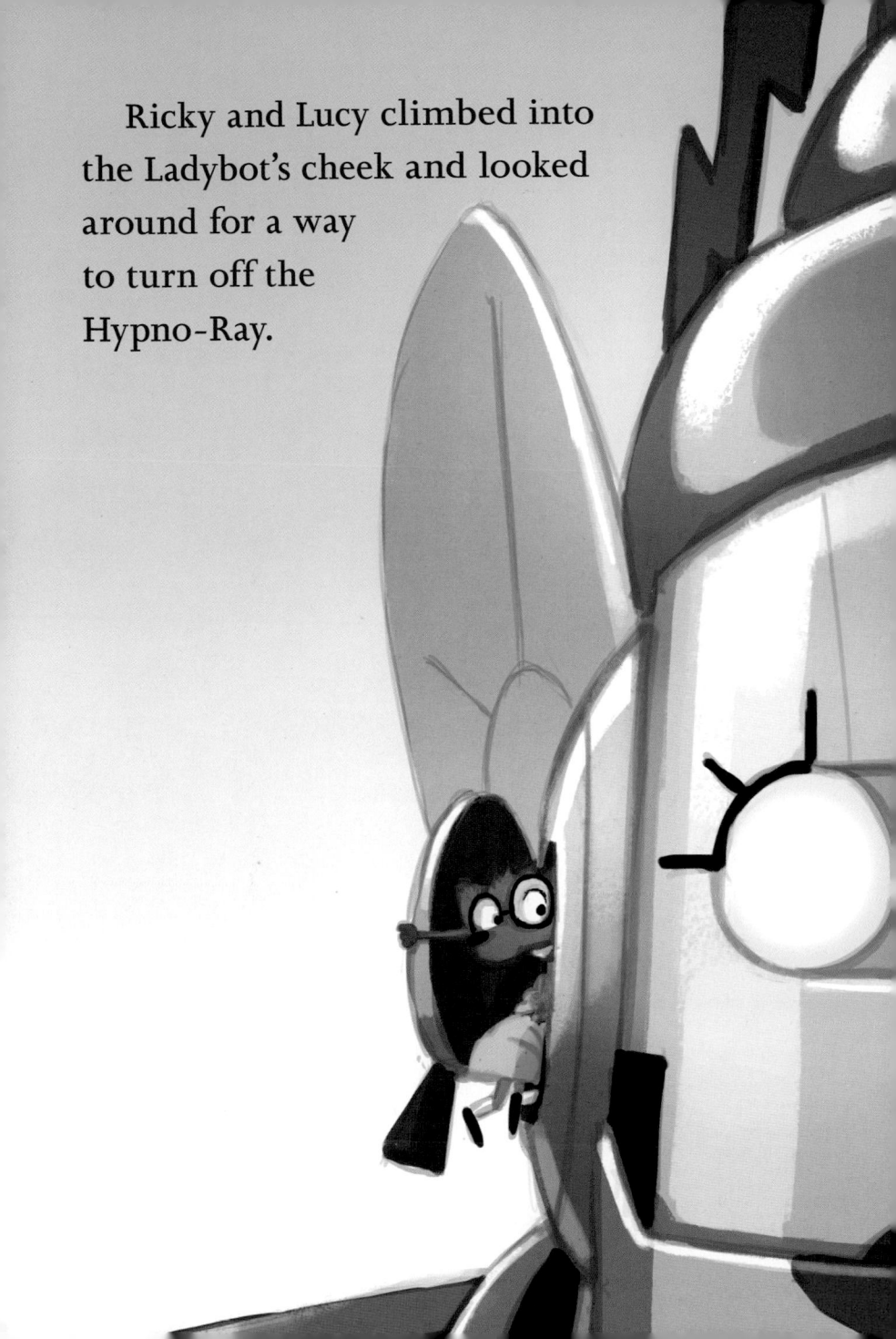

Suddenly, Uncle Unicorn found Ricky and Lucy.

"So, you thought you could save the day, huh?" laughed Uncle Unicorn. "Well, you were WRONG!" Uncle Unicorn tied up Ricky and Lucy and hung them high above the main generator.

Ricky looked down. "If only
there were some way I could
destroy that generator," said
Ricky. "But how?"

CHAPTER NINE
THE GENERATOR

Just then, a few drops of sweat
dripped from Ricky's face. They fell
down into the generator. Suddenly,
a giant spark flashed out of the
generator, followed by a puff of black
smoke. The generator stopped for a
split second, then continued running.

"A-*HA*!" cried Ricky. "If I can get
that generator wet, it will shut down!"
Ricky tried to sweat more, but he
couldn't. He tried to spit into the
generator, but his mouth was too dry.

"Lucy," said Ricky, "you've got to spit down onto that generator!"

"No way!" said Lucy. "Princesses do NOT spit!"

"*Pleeeeease?*" Ricky begged. "It's a matter of life and death!" But Lucy still refused.

Then, Ricky got a sneaky idea.

"Just think," said Ricky. "If those Unicorns destroy the planet, there will be no more ice cream and no more chocolate chip cookies . . ."

"N-n-no more ice cream?" Lucy whimpered. Her eyes welled up with tears. "N-n-no more chocolate chip cookies?"

Giant teardrops began dripping down Lucy's face.

"And no more cotton candy and coconut cream pie," said Ricky. "And no more vanilla wafers and grape lollipops."

"N-n-no m-m-more g-g-grape lollipops?" cried Lucy.

Suddenly, Lucy burst into tears. Giant tears sprayed from her face and fell down into the generator below.

Bright sparks and horrible black smoke began shooting out of the generator. It shook back and forth. Then, finally, it broke down.

"Hooray!" shouted Ricky.

CHAPTER TEN
RICKY'S ROBOT RETURNS

The generator was broken, the Ladybot had shut down, and the Hypno-Ray had stopped working. Suddenly, Ricky's Mighty Robot returned to normal.

The Mighty Robot did not know
where he was, or what was going on,
but he knew he had to save the day.

With a mighty burst of Robo-Power,
Ricky's Robot snapped his chains. Then,
they all started to fight.

The big, bad beasties banded together and blasted the Robot's behind.

So Ricky's Robot unleashed an
ultra-unbeatable Unicorn uppercut.

Then the plucky protector prevailed by punching the putrid ponies into a perilous pile-up.

The Uranium Unicorns were very angry.

"No more horsing around," they said. "It's time to kick some Robot tushy!"

CHAPTER ELEVEN
THE BIG BATTLE
(IN FLIP-O-RAMA™)

-RAMA

HERE'S HOW IT WORKS!

STEP 1

Place your *left* hand inside
the dotted lines marked
"LEFT HAND HERE."
Hold the book open *flat*.

STEP 2

Grasp the *right-hand* page with
your right thumb and index finger
(inside the dotted lines marked
"RIGHT THUMB HERE").

STEP 3

Now *quickly* flip the right-
hand page back and forth
until the picture appears
to be *animated*.

(For extra fun, try adding your own sound-effects!)

FLIP-O-RAMA 1

(pages 77 and 79)

Remember, flip *only* page 77.
While you are flipping, be sure you
can see the picture on page 77
and the one on page 79.
If you flip quickly, the two
pictures will start to look like
<u>one</u> *animated* picture.

Don't forget to add
your own sound-effects!

LEFT HAND HERE

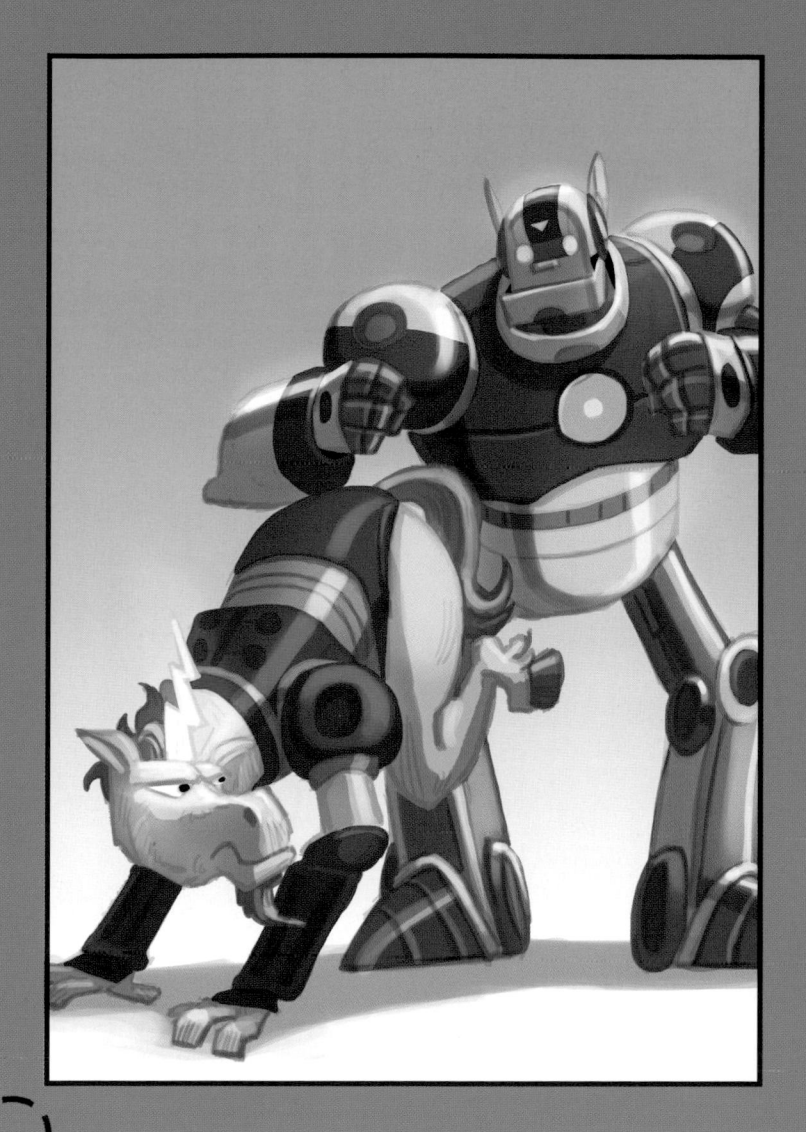

THE URANIUM UNICORNS ATTACKED.

RIGHT
THUMB
HERE

THE URANIUM UNICORNS ATTACKED.

FLIP-O-RAMA 2

(pages 81 and 83)

Remember, flip *only* page 81.
While you are flipping, be sure you
can see the picture on page 81
and the one on page 83.
If you flip quickly, the two
pictures will start to look like
<u>one</u> *animated* picture.

Don't forget to add
your own sound-effects!

LEFT HAND HERE

RICKY'S MIGHTY ROBOT
FOUGHT BACK.

RIGHT
THUMB
HERE

RIGHT
INDEX
FINGER
HERE

RICKY'S MIGHTY ROBOT
FOUGHT BACK.

FLIP-O-RAMA 3

(pages 85 and 87)

Remember, flip *only* page 85.
While you are flipping, be sure you
can see the picture on page 85
and the one on page 87.
If you flip quickly, the two
pictures will start to look like
<u>one</u> *animated* picture.

Don't forget to add
your own sound-effects!

LEFT HAND HERE

THE URANIUM UNICORNS
BATTLED HARD.

RIGHT
THUMB
HERE

RIGHT INDEX FINGER HERE

**THE URANIUM UNICORNS
BATTLED HARD.**

FLIP-O-RAMA 4

(pages 89 and 91)

Remember, flip only page 89.
While you are flipping, be sure you
can see the picture on page 89
and the one on page 91.
If you flip quickly, the two
pictures will start to look like
<u>one</u> *animated* picture.

Don't forget to add
your own sound-effects!

LEFT HAND HERE

RICKY'S MIGHTY ROBOT
BATTLED HARDER.

RIGHT
INDEX
FINGER
HERE

**RICKY'S MIGHTY ROBOT
BATTLED HARDER.**

FLIP-O-RAMA 5

(pages 93 and 95)

Remember, flip *only* page 93.
While you are flipping, be sure you
can see the picture on page 93
and the one on page 95.
If you flip quickly, the two
pictures will start to look like
<u>one</u> *animated* picture.

Don't forget to add
your own sound-effects!

LEFT HAND HERE

RICKY'S MIGHTY ROBOT
WON THE WAR.

RIGHT
THUMB
HERE

RIGHT INDEX FINGER HERE

RICKY'S MIGHTY ROBOT
WON THE WAR.

CHAPTER TWELVE
THE SUPER MECHA-EVIL LADYBOT

Ricky's Mighty Robot had defeated the Uranium Unicorns, but Uncle Unicorn was not ready to give up just yet.

Quickly, he turned on the backup generator, and then he pressed a secret button on his control panel.

FINALLY, THE MIGHTY ROBOT REACHED A STEEP MOUNTAIN.

THERE WAS NO PLACE LEFT TO RUN.

THE LADYBOT TRIED TO LIFT HER MASSIVE FOOT...

...AND CAME CRASHING TO THE GROUND.

WHAM!

Ricky and Lucy untied their ropes and ran out of the Ladybot's cheek.

Uncle Unicorn chased after them . . .

. . . but Ricky's Mighty Robot stopped him just in time.

"My beautiful Ladybot is destroyed!" cried Uncle Unicorn. "How did it happen?"

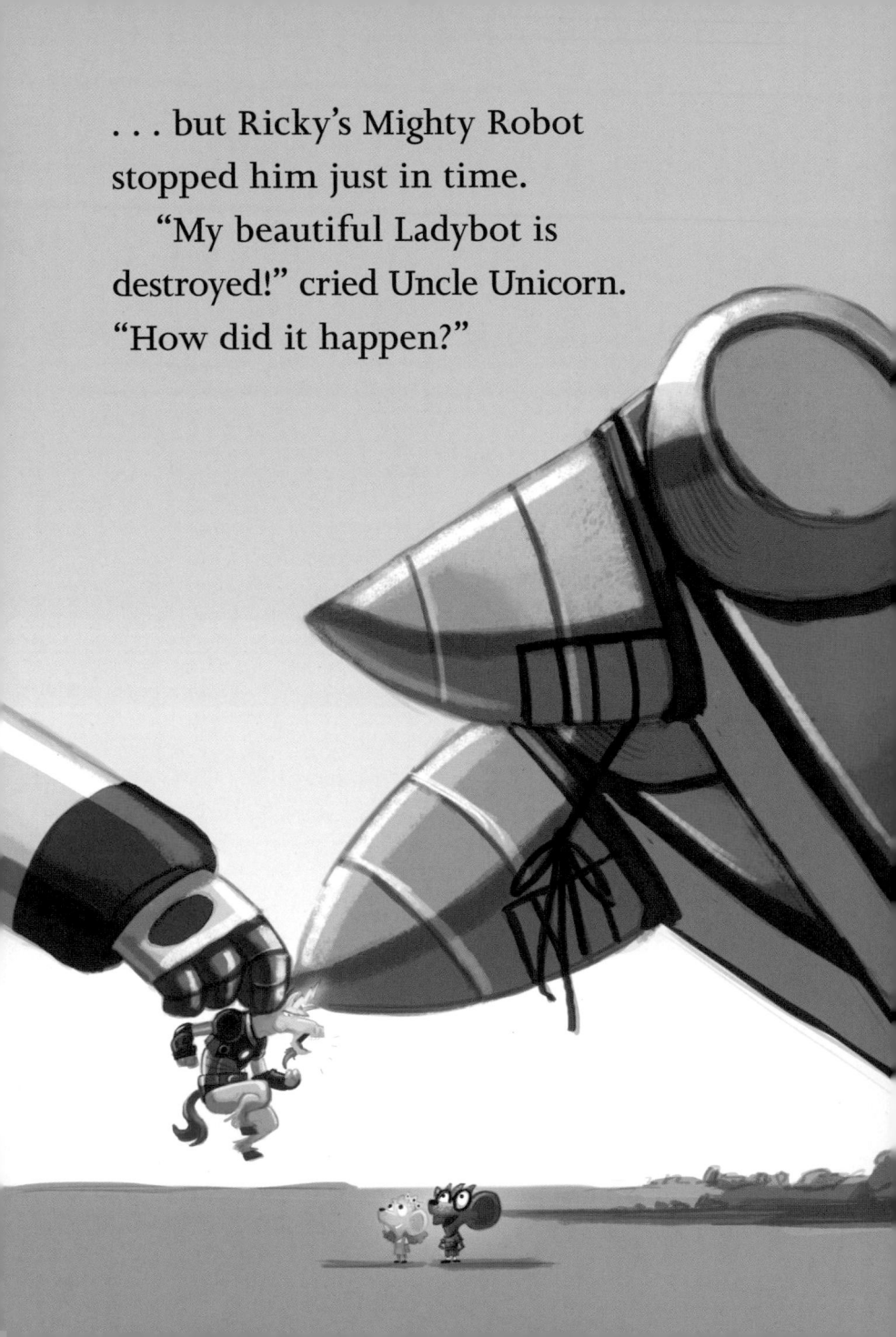

"It looks like somebody tied her shoelaces together," said Ricky.

"But who could have done that?" asked Lucy.

Just then, Fudgie and Cupcake poked their heads out of the bushes. They had been helpful after all.

"Hooray for Fudgie and Cupcake!" cried Lucy.

YOU DIDN'T EAT THEM, DID YOU?

WELL??

WHERE ARE THEY THEN?

BLEEEAH

EWW...

YOU GUYS ARE DISGUSTING!

CHAPTER THIRTEEN
JUSTICE PREVAILS

Ricky's Mighty Robot stuffed the three Uranium Unicorns into their rocket ship and threw it back to Uranus.

Then he picked up the giant
Ladybot and threw her back, too.

117

Finally, they all took
Uncle Unicorn to the
Squeakyville jail, which
was getting very crowded.

Ricky and his Mighty Robot flew Lucy and her Jurassic Jackrabbits back to their house.

"Do you want to stay and play *princess?*" asked Lucy.

"No, thanks," said Ricky. "I've got something important to do!"

And, together, the two friends flew home.

CHAPTER FOURTEEN
BEDTIME

That night after supper, Ricky helped his Mighty Robot get ready for bed.

Ricky brushed his Mighty Robot's giant teeth . . .

. . . then he helped his Mighty
Robot put on his pajamas . . .

. . . and, finally, he tucked his
Mighty Robot into bed.

"I'm glad you boys are having fun again," said Ricky's father, "even though you are both very different."
"Me, too," said Ricky . . .

. . . "that's what friends are for."

READY FOR

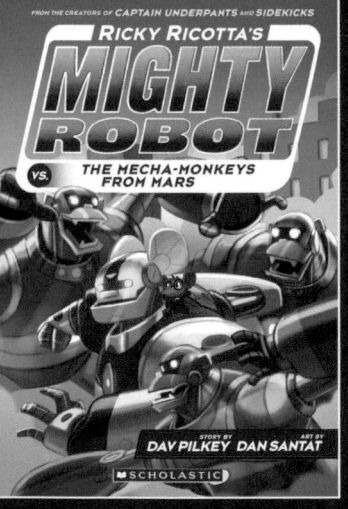